Riley
the Skateboarding
Fairy

Join the **Rainbow Magic Reading Challenge!**

Read the story and collect your fairy points to climb the Reading Rainbow at the back of the book.

This book is worth 1 star.

To Hettie and Maddie, true friends of the fairies!

Special thanks to
Rachel Elliot

ORCHARD BOOKS

First published in Great Britain in 2021 by The Watts Publishing Group

3 5 7 9 10 8 6 4 2

A CIP catalogue record for this book is available from the British Library.

ISBN 978 1 40836 448 2

Printed and bound in Great Britain by Clays Ltd, Elcograf S.p.A

The paper and board used in this book are made from wood from responsible sources.

Orchard Books
An imprint of Hachette Children's Group
Part of The Watts Publishing Group Limited
Carmelite House, 50 Victoria Embankment, London EC4Y 0DZ

An Hachette UK Company
www.hachette.co.uk
www.hachettechildrens.co.uk

Riley the Skateboarding Fairy

By Daisy Meadows

ORCHARD

www.orchardseriesbooks.co.uk

Fairyland Palace
Surfing Festival
Port Pearl Beach
Skate Park
Youth Hostel

Jack Frost's Ice Castle
Goblin Grotto
Mistfall Mountains
Silverlake Valley
Dewbelle Ski Resort

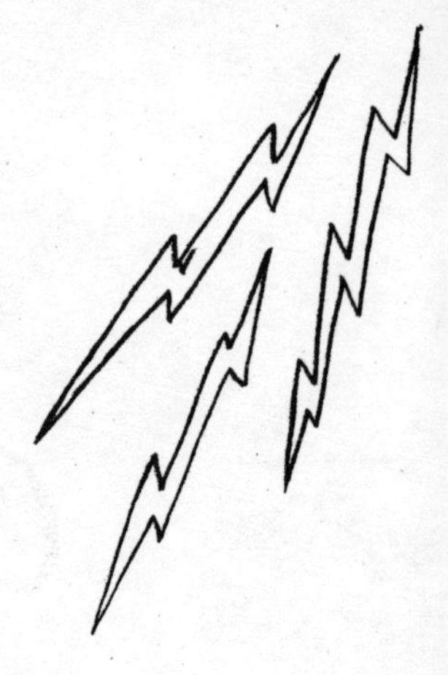

Jack Frost's Ode

Each goody-goody fairy pest
Says 'Never cheat' and 'Try your best'.
Their words should end up in the bin.
To be the best you have to win!

I'll steal and cheat to find a way
Of winning every game I play,
And when the world is at my feet
They'll see it's always best to cheat!

Contents

"Wasn't it fun meeting Layne yesterday?" said Rachel. "I wonder if we'll see Riley the Skateboarding Fairy today."

As well as competing in the Gold Medal Games, the girls had shared an amazing fairy adventure. They had saved Layne the Surfing Fairy's magical surfboard from Jack Frost, who had disguised himself as a surfer called Lightning Jack and nearly ruined the first Gold Medal Games competition. In a fury, Jack Frost had sent his goblins to steal special things from the other Gold Medal Games Fairies. If they had succeeded, today's skateboarding competition might be in big trouble.

"There it is," said Kirsty, as they reached the top of the sand dunes. "Wow,

it's so big!"

The concrete skatepark was divided into four separate areas. The first was made up of curving quarter pipes. The second had a mini ramp, a flat bank and a curved ledge. Next was a simple staircase, and the fourth section looked like a giant bowl carved into the ground.

"It makes me feel a bit nervous to think of skateboarding here in front of crowds

of people," said Rachel.

"Do you remember what Layne taught us about playing a sport?" Kirsty said. "It isn't about winning or doing well. It's about enjoying yourself."

They shared a smile and hurried down the slope to the skatepark.

"I wish we could find out what happened in Fairyland yesterday," said Rachel, worriedly.

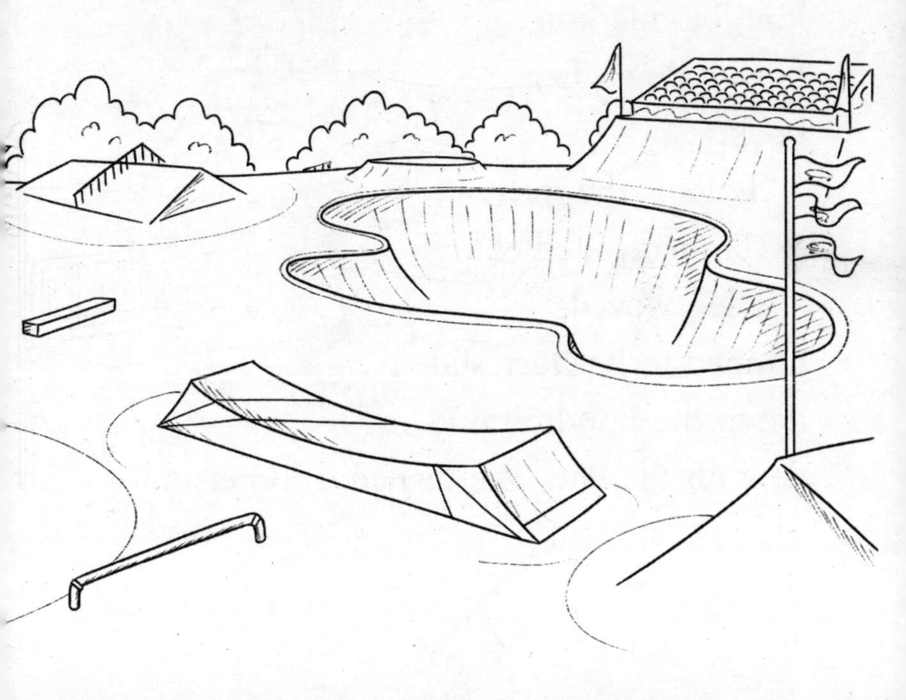

"Sometimes, wishes are granted," said a silvery voice beside them.

They whirled around and saw Riley the Skateboarding Fairy sitting on the handrail of the staircase. She was wearing a tie-dye T-shirt, a denim jacket and shorts. Her pink kneepads and elbow-pads matched her pink helmet, and her long blonde hair flowed down her back.

"Riley!" the girls exclaimed together.

Riley waved, jumped to her feet, slid down the handrail and flew off the end. She turned a somersault

and bowed as she fluttered in midair. Rachel and Kirsty laughed and clapped.

"I wish I could do tricks like that," said Rachel. "You can even do them without a skateboard!"

"I have never let my disability hold me back from being the best skateboarder I can be," said Riley. "Losing my skateboard isn't going to stop me!"

The girls' smiles faded.

"Did the goblins take it?" asked Rachel.

"Yes, and that's why I'm here," said Riley. "I need your help to get it back."

Chapter Two
A Suspicious Skateboarder

"We know that Lightning Jack told his goblins to steal your things," said Rachel. "What happened?"

"I was watching over the Surfing Festival with Soraya the Skiing Fairy and Jayda the Snowboarding Fairy," said Riley, fluttering down to perch on the

handrail. "We left our magical objects behind one of the stalls. Then the goblins came and turned everything upside down. It was only after they ran away that we realised they must have taken our magical objects with them. Now I can't do my job, and I'm scared that today's competition is going to be a big flop."

"I'm so sorry," said Rachel. "Please tell us about your job."

"I look after skateboarders in the human and fairy worlds," Riley explained. "I make sure that they develop their skills, and help them to accept all kinds of people. Skateboarding is all about including everyone."

"It sounds as if Lightning Jack is going to be included today," said Kirsty with a sigh. "We have to get your magical

skateboard away from him to save the competition."

At that moment, Rachel noticed that they were not alone in the skatepark. A young woman with curly red hair was sitting on top of the ramp, staring into the distance. Beside her was a black skateboard with a bright red flame down the middle.

"Who's that?" Rachel asked.

Riley immediately darted into Kirsty's pocket.

"That's Lana Cassidy," she said. "She is one of the best skateboarders in the world. You should go over and say hi. She's super cool."

Rachel and Kirsty walked over to the young woman.

"Good morning," said Kirsty.

"Hello," the woman said in a friendly voice. "I'm Lana. Are you taking part in the competition today?"

The girls nodded, and Kirsty stepped forward.

"I'm Kirsty and this is my friend Rachel," she said. "We came to see where we'll be skateboarding later on."

"This is a special place," said Lana, gazing around. "It's where I learned how to skateboard."

"Did you grow up here?" Rachel asked.

"Yes, and it's lovely to be back," said Lana. "I travel all around the world, but there's nowhere quite like home."

"Are you coming to watch the competition?" asked Kirsty.

"Definitely," said Lana with a laugh. "I'm one of the judges! I'd love to see

what you can do. Here, use my board."

She handed her black-and-red board to Kirsty, who opened her eyes wide.

"You mean – right now?"

"There's no time like the present," said Lana.

Kirsty gulped and took the board. Feeling nervous and excited at the same time, she pushed off and carved around the section, kickturning to make a tight turn. She jumped down

two steps and ground the board to a stop with the tail.

"Not bad at all!" said Lana. "You've got great balance, Kirsty. Make sure you slide the side of your foot up the board when you do that trick."

Next, Rachel whizzed around the skatepark and tried to do a trick called a kickflip. Lana clapped and whistled.

"That was awesome, Rachel!" she called. "Just make sure you're kicking your leg outwards and upwards."

Rachel returned the skateboard, panting and smiling.

"Thanks for the tips," said Kirsty.

Lana started to speak, but her voice was drowned out by a loud, boastful voice behind them.

"I'm the best of the best," said the sharp

voice. "Everyone else might as well give up now."

Lana, Rachel and Kirsty turned around and saw Lightning Jack in a backwards baseball cap. There were three goblins with him, all wearing sideways green caps and shiny tracksuits.

"Keep out of the way," Lightning Jack ordered the goblins. "I'm so amazingly fast that you could get knocked down."

He was wearing a dark blue T-shirt with a gold flash of lightning on the front, a pair of baggy shorts and shiny white hi-tops. His hair poked out from under his cap, tied into a rough bun. A blue-and-pink skateboard was tucked under his arm, and Kirsty felt Riley wriggle in her pocket. Could that be the magical skateboard?

Chapter Three
A Fairy Prisoner

"Clear the skatepark," Jack Frost barked at Lana and the girls. "I'm Lightning Jack, and I need to practise. Clear off. You'll never win anyway."

Lana shook her head at Lightning Jack.

"You know, you might be a better skateboarder if you were a bit less

interested in yourself, and a bit kinder to other people," she said. "Friendship between competitors is important and truly successful sportspeople value it. Skateboarding is all about being yourself and accepting others for who they are."

"Huh, what would you know?" scoffed Lightning Jack.

Lana gave a little smile.

"I'm a champion skateboarder and I'm one of the judges of the competition today," she said, turning to leave. "But don't let that worry you. I'm very fair. See you later, girls."

Rachel and Kirsty had to giggle when they saw Lightning Jack's surprised face. The goblins stuck out their tongues.

"Stop hanging around here," the tallest goblin squawked. "Go and pester someone else."

Lightning Jack pushed off and whizzed around the skatepark, performing the most complicated jumps and tricks that the girls had ever seen.

"He looks as if he's flying," said Kirsty.

Riley peeped out of her pocket.

"It's all because of my board," she said.

"He's using all its magic to make himself the best, so there's no magic left to take care of all the other skateboarders."

"All you need to do is touch the skateboard," said Rachel. "Magical items return to fairy size as soon as their owner touches them. Do you think you could do it while he's riding?"

It was still early and there was no one else in sight.

"I'll give it a try!" said Riley in a determined voice.

She shot out of Kirsty's pocket and zoomed after Lightning Jack, leaping and flipping through the air as she followed his moves on the skateboard.

"A fairy!" squealed the smallest goblin. "Look out!"

"Bigspin three-sixty kickflip!" yelled

Lightning Frost.

He did a full turn, and Riley flew straight into his hands.

"No!" cried Rachel.

It was too late. Lightning Jack had trapped Riley in his bony hands.

"Do what I say and leave me alone," he said, glaring at the girls.

Kirsty stepped forward, feeling too worried about her friend to be afraid.

"Let her go," she insisted. "Why are you doing this?"

"I'm going to be famous," said Lightning Jack. "Sports stars get all the attention, and I'm going to be the biggest sports star of all. Children will be easy to beat, especially with my magic skateboard. So stop pestering me."

"Using magic to win is like cheating," said Kirsty. "How can you be happy to win by cheating?"

Lightning Jack shrugged his shoulders.

"I don't care as long as I win," he said. "Winning is all that matters. It means I'm the best."

"Please let Riley go," said Rachel.

Lightning Jack cackled with laughter and turned away, with the tiny fairy trapped in his hands.

"We have to save Riley and get the skateboard away from Lightning Jack before the competition is ruined," said Kirsty.

"There's no way we can get near him right now," said Rachel. "He's watching

us and the event stewards are starting to arrive. Let's go and have some breakfast. Hopefully we can think of a plan before the competition starts."

When the girls arrived back at the youth hostel, it was buzzing with chatter and excitement about the day ahead. Rachel and Kirsty sat down for breakfast with Kirsty's schoolfriends.

"Rachel, this is Sean Plum," said Kirsty, introducing a boy with curly black hair. "He's Wetherbury's best hope for the skateboarding gold medal."

"Thanks," said Sean with a grin. "I've loved every minute of learning to skateboard, but I'm most excited about meeting Lana Cassidy. Did you hear that

she is going to be one of the judges?"

"Oh, we just met her!" said Rachel.

Sean went pink with excitement.

"I wish I'd been there," he said with longing. "I'm her biggest fan. I've even started a 'We love Lana Cassidy' club."

Suddenly, Rachel had an idea.

"Maybe if Lightning Jack thought he had a fan club, he would let us get close

to him," she whispered to Kirsty. "I know we tried being superfans at the surfing event, but if we put on good disguises I think it could work."

"We have to try," Kirsty agreed. "Poor Riley is in danger and we have to save her and the magical skateboard."

While everyone else was collecting their skateboards, Rachel and Kirsty changed into baggy clothes and pulled caps low

over their faces. Rachel found a roll of paper and made some banners that said "Go Lightning!" on them. Kirsty made large badges decorated with Lightning Jack's face. Each of them took their camera, a notebook for autographs and a pen.

"Do you think he'll recognise us?" asked Rachel.

Kirsty looked at her and giggled.

"Even *I* don't recognise you," she said. "I really think that this is going to work."

Chapter Four

Praising Jack

They headed back to the skatepark. It was no longer quiet and peaceful. Rows of seats had been set up around the skatepark, with three chairs for the judges. Crowds of people were arriving to watch the competition. Skateboarders were whizzing in all directions, getting

some last-minute practice before the start of the competition. It didn't take long to spot Lightning Jack.

"That was a one-eighty," he was telling three goblins in shiny tracksuits. "Now watch what I do next!"

He zoomed off, tick-tacking, kickflipping and showing off on the ramps. The goblins only watched for a couple of seconds before a quarrel broke out. Lightning Jack flipped his skateboard into his hand and stomped over to where the goblins were sitting.

"You weren't watching!" he shouted at them.

"*We* were," Kirsty exclaimed, rushing forward with her pen and notebook. "Could we have your autograph?"

"We think you're amazing," added

Rachel. "That was the best frontside powerslide I've ever seen."

They had both disguised their voices and kept their heads down. Lightning Jack gave a conceited smile and scribbled his name in Kirsty's notebook.

"That's how proper fans behave," he shouted at the goblins. "You should be watching everything I do and holding up banners. Give me more praise. I'M THE BEST!"

The goblins scowled and slumped in their seats, folding their arms.

"Make room for my superfans," said Lightning Jack. "Budge up!"

The girls sat in between the goblins and Lightning Jack.

"I wonder if they're keeping Riley prisoner under these seats," Rachel whispered into Kirsty's ear.

Kirsty tried to peep under her seat, but at that moment everyone burst into applause. The judges had taken their seats. Lana was in the middle, holding a microphone.

"Welcome to the Gold Medal Games skateboarding event," she announced. "Each competitor will have three runs around the skatepark – that's three chances to impress us with your skills. We'll be awarding marks out of one hundred, and we're looking out for great flow, originality and creativity. Use as much of the course as possible, and have fun. The first competitor is . . . Sean Plum. Get ready, Sean!"

At the far end of the skatepark, the girls saw Sean grin happily and put his helmet on.

"Why is *he* first?" Lightning Jack complained. "It should be me."

"You're right," said Rachel. "It's terrible that they don't realise how amazing you are."

Lightning Jack nodded, and the girls exchanged a little smile. Their plan was working. Getting close to Lightning Jack was their best chance of finding Riley.

Sean Plum dropped into the bowl and immediately fell off his skateboard. Lightning Jack laughed loudly.

"Poor Sean," whispered Kirsty.

He got up again and kept going, but he lost his balance on the next trick and tumbled into the bottom of the bowl.

"What a nincompoop," said Lightning Jack.

Kirsty desperately wanted to stand up for her friend, but she had to play the part of a superfan. Then other voices started calling out from the crowd.

"Rubbish."

"Poor."

"Boring."

Sean went bright red. By the end of his run, he had only managed to do one trick without falling or wobbling.

"I'm sure that skateboarding audiences aren't usually so mean," said Rachel in Kirsty's ear. "It must be because the

magical skateboard has been stolen."

Kirsty nodded, and a worried frown crinkled her forehead.

"Great start, Sean," said Lana with an encouraging grin. "It's hard to go first, and I know you'll pull off some of those harder tricks off next time when you're more relaxed. You've earned forty-nine points. Next up, it's Lightning Jack."

Rachel and Kirsty whooped and cheered as Lightning Jack made his way to the bowl. He nudged the tip of Riley's skateboard over the edge.

"This is going to be the most amazing thing you've ever seen," he yelled.

Lightning Jack gave a superb performance. People were leaping out of their seats and cheering as he did trick after amazing trick. The girls didn't dare search for Riley with everyone jumping around. When Lightning Jack had finished, the crowd went wild.

"An awesome first run from newcomer Lightning Jack," said Lana into the microphone. "There was so much creative content, we judges were truly amazed. You've earned ninety-five points. I'm sure next time we'll see that extra something

that will gain you full marks."

Lightning Jack stomped back towards the girls and the goblins. He was scowling horribly.

"That stupid judge doesn't know how to do her stupid job," he raged. "How dare she not give me full marks? I am brilliant and perfect."

Rachel remembered that both Lana and Layne the Surfing Fairy had said that in their sports, people who were only interested in their own skills and abilities could never truly succeed.

"I'm going to freeze the lot of them," Lightning Jack hissed to the goblins. "Then I can change the score to one hundred and be the winner."

The goblins laughed and rubbed their hands together, and a cold, grey mist started to swirl around Lightning Jack. Rachel and Kirsty glanced at each other in alarm. They had to stop him before the whole day was ruined.

Chapter Five
Litterbugs

Kirsty had a sudden brainwave.

"Over here!" she shouted in her loudest voice. "The best skateboarder in the competition is right here. Come and meet the amazing Lightning Jack. Grab your cameras!"

Almost instantly, there was a small

crowd of admirers around Lightning Jack. He stopped scowling as people shook his hand, took his picture and showered him with praise. Soon he was preening like a peacock and the grey mist receeded.

"This skateboard is getting in my way," he said, shoving it into the arms of one of the goblins. "Look after it. My fans need me."

Rachel and Kirsty watched as the goblins skipped away from the park towards the sand dunes.

"Let's look for Riley," said Kirsty. "Then we can try to catch up with the goblins."

With Lightning Jack hidden behind a wall of fans, the girls were able to race to the seats without being noticed. Would Riley be hidden under there?

The only things under the seats were

empty sweet wrappers and crisp packets. There was no sign of the little fairy. The girls shared a look of dismay.

"I don't understand," said Kirsty. "I felt sure Lightning Jack would want to keep Riley nearby."

"Where else could he have hidden her?" asked Rachel.

"Perhaps he took her to the Ice Castle," Kirsty said.

Absentmindedly, she started to pick up the litter that Lightning Jack and the goblins had dropped. Rachel knelt down to help.

"Oh, there's something in this crisp packet," she exclaimed.

It was tied with an elastic band, and it felt strangely heavy in the palm of her hand. They looked into each other's shining eyes.

"Could it be . . . ?" Rachel said.

Kirsty pulled the elastic band off. Yes! Riley

fluttered out, brushing crisp crumbs off her clothes.

"Thank you," she said with relief. "I knew you'd find me. My wand is in one of the other bags. Please help me find it."

The girls shook every crisp packet upside down, until at last a tiny wand tumbled out, sprinkling fairy dust among the crisp crumbs.

"Thank goodness you decided to tidy up," Riley exclaimed.

While Rachel put the litter in a nearby bin, Kirsty glanced around.

"Lightning Jack is in that crowd, and the goblins have gone off with your skateboard," she said. "Hide in my pocket and we'll go after them."

"I've got a better idea," said Riley. "We can follow the goblins more quickly if

we're all fairies."

Eagerly, Rachel and Kirsty ducked down behind the seats where no one could see them. Riley raised her wand.

"To help you fly without a care,
I give you wings as light as air."

A whoosh of sparkling fairy dust lifted the girls off their feet and shrank them to fairy size. Shimmering wings of rose gold lifted them high above the crowds. Rachel twirled joyfully, swooping and diving around her friends.

"This is how birds must feel," she said. "Just glad to be alive!"

Riley hugged them both, and then pointed to the sand dunes.

"I think I can see the goblins," she said.

"Let's go."

Over the brow of the hill, the goblins were very busy. They had turned Riley's magical skateboard upside down, and they were trying to sand surf. It wasn't going well.

"It's my turn," the tallest goblin yelled, snatching the skateboard from the smallest goblin.

"Liar liar, pants on fire," said the smallest goblin, blowing a raspberry.

The fairies flew down and hid among the long grasses. They watched as the tall goblin pushed off, flipped over and landed on his head.

"Is that what sand surfing is supposed to look like?" asked Kirsty.

"No," said Riley firmly. "Sand surfing needs a completely different type of board, and it wouldn't work in these dunes anyway. All they're going to do is hurt themselves and damage my skateboard."

The goblins eventually realised this. They flopped down on the sand, looking grumpy.

"This is boring," said the middle goblin.

"Watching Lightning Jack isn't much fun either," said the smallest goblin.

"I'd rather be playing beach ball," said the tallest goblin.

The loudspeakers whined and echoed from the skatepark.

"We are pausing the competition for a few minutes to check the name lists," said Lana's voice. "I'm sorry about all the confusion, folks. Please be patient."

"It sounds as if they're having problems," said Kirsty. "Lightning Jack will soon be wondering where we and the goblins have gone."

"We have to hurry," said Rachel. "It's a shame they're lying down. If they were distracted, they might not notice Riley trying to touch the skateboard."

"That's it!" said Kirsty, giving a little jump of excitement. "Riley, can you make us human again and give us beach clothes and lots of balls? If they want to play a game, they shall!"

Riley grinned and waved her wand. At least twenty beach balls plopped down on to the surprised goblins. Rachel and Kirsty, now human again, ran out from their hiding places. They were wearing tankinis and big sunhats that hid their faces.

"Hello!" said Rachel, waving at the goblins. "Anyone for beach ball?"

Chapter Six
A Barmy Ball Game

"This is the most bonkers beach ball game ever," said Rachel, a few minutes later.

Goblins and beach balls were flying left, right and centre. Balls were bouncing off heads, zooming over dunes and occasionally bursting when a goblin

landed on them. The tallest goblin had tucked the magical skateboard under his arm.

"Catch!" shouted Kirsty, hurling a ball at him and hoping he would drop the skateboard.

"Yikes!" squawked the goblin.

Flustered, he tried to kick the ball with both feet and fell on to his back. The other goblins shrieked with laughter.

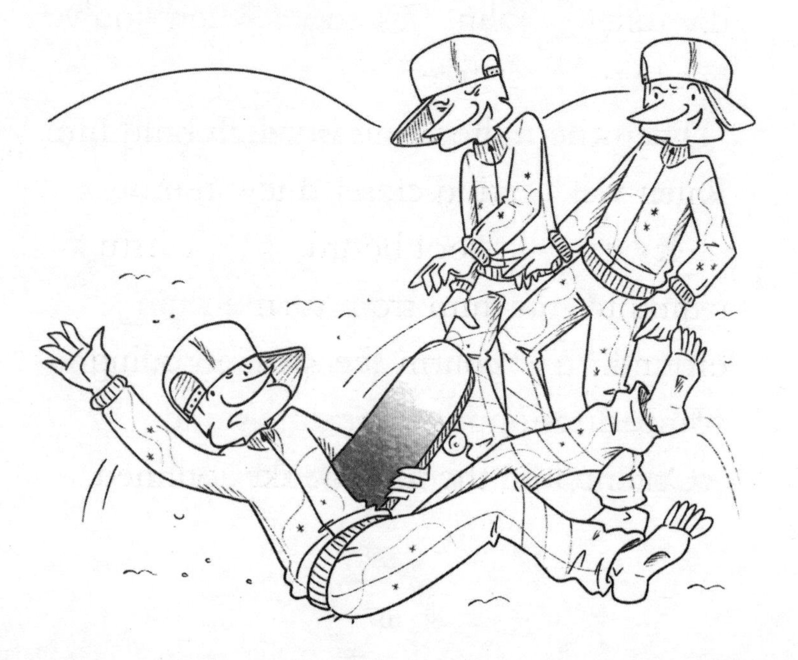

The loudspeaker crackled again.

"I'm sorry, but we have another problem," said Lana's voice. "We're a bit unlucky this morning for some reason! Please bear with us while we sort this out."

The beach balls kept coming, and Kirsty spotted Riley slipping among the tall grasses towards her skateboard.

"Why not put that down?" she called to the tallest goblin. "It's easier when you've got two hands free."

The goblin shook his head. Behind him, Riley was getting closer and closer.

"It's a really cool board," said Kirsty, trying to stop him from turning around. "Are you in the skateboarding competition?"

Once again the loudspeaker whined.

"This is a message for Lightning Jack's assistants," said Lana. "Please return to the skatepark with his skateboard. He is feeling a little . . . impatient."

The goblin turned to go. Riley flew into the open, stretching her hand towards her skateboard. Then Lightning Jack appeared over the top of the sand dunes.

"Look behind you, idiot!" he yelled at the goblin.

The goblin saw Riley, panicked and threw the skateboard away from him as hard as he could.

"Stop her!" Lightning Jack bellowed.

The goblins and Riley chased after the skateboard, but the goblins tripped over the scattered beach balls. Riley's hand touched the edge of the skateboard and

it instantly returned to fairy size. In one fluid movement, she flipped it into the air and rode it upwards.

"Yes!" the girls cheered, throwing their hats into the air.

Lightning Jack flung his baseball cap on the ground and stamped on it.

"I'm not beaten yet!" he yelled. "The winter Gold Medal Games Fairies are finished. Winter is MINE, and I've got lots of time to make a

plan that you'll never be able to foil. I'm going to be a world-famous sports star, and you can't stop me!"

There was a crackle of blue lightning, and Jack Frost disappeared with the goblins, who were still clutching their beach balls. Riley flew down to the girls, beaming her biggest smile.

"We did it!" she whooped, flipping her board and punching the air. "Yes! Thank you, girls. Without you, I'd still be trapped in that crisp packet."

"We're so happy we could help," said Kirsty.

"I'm going back to Fairyland to tell the news to the other Gold Medal Games Fairies," said Riley. "But before I go . . ."

She waved her wand, and the girls were briefly wrapped in glittering fairy dust. When the sparkles faded, they were wearing new skateboarding outfits and helmets.

"Thank you!" they said.

Riley waved and vanished in a starry twinkle. The loudspeaker crackled again.

"Could Kirsty Tate of Wetherbury School make her way to the bowl for her

first run?" said Lana.

Rachel grabbed her best friend's hand. "Come on," she said. "It's time to ride!"

Later, in the hazy afternoon sun, Lana Cassidy placed the gold medal around Sean Plum's neck.

"We were super-impressed by your attitude and ability," she said. "After a shaky start, you could have lost confidence and given up. But you kept believing in yourself, and it paid off. Congratulations!"

The skatepark rang with cheers, and the girls shared a happy smile.

"This has been the best weekend ever," said Kirsty. "The only trouble is, I can't decide if I like surfing or skateboarding best!"

"It's been great," Rachel agreed. "But I can't stop thinking about what Lightning Jack said. He still has Jayda and Soraya's special objects."

"He is not going to succeed," said Kirsty. "After all, if he has lots of time to prepare a plan, so do we!"

"And we've got each other," said Rachel. "Best friends make the best team ever!"

The End

Now it's time for Kirsty and Rachel to help...

Olympia the Games Fairy

Read on for a sneak peek...

"This is going to be really exciting!" Kirsty Tate said, beaming at her best friend, Rachel Walker. Kirsty had just arrived in Tippington to stay with Rachel for part of the summer holidays. "It's the first time I've ever been to a – a—" Kirsty stopped, looking confused. "*What* did you say this sporting event was called, Rachel?"

Her friend laughed. "A triathlon," she reminded Kirsty as Mr Walker turned the car down a street signposted *To the river.* "All the athletes take part in swimming, cycling and running races, one after the other. They don't even get a break in between! That's right, isn't it, Mum?"

"Yes," replied Mrs Walker from the passenger seat. "They go from one event straight into the next."

Kirsty's eyes opened wide. "Wow, they must be super-fit!" she exclaimed.

"I think we're going to be exhausted just cheering them on," joked Mr Walker, who was now searching for an empty space in the packed car park.

The triathlon was taking place in the pretty riverside town of Melford, not far from Tippington. As they all climbed out of the car, Kirsty admired the little thatched cottages and the stone-built church with its square belltower. It was a perfect summer's day with a brilliant-blue sky and sunshine streaming down.

"There are loads of people here," Rachel remarked, as they followed the crowds down the street. Ahead of them the girls could see a long waterfront with an ancient stone bridge spanning the wide river. A set of steps led down to the edge of the river, and there were men and women in swimming costumes and colourful swimming caps standing on the steps, waiting eagerly for the race to start.

Read *Olympia the Games Fairy* to find out what adventures are in store for Kirsty and Rachel!

Calling all parents, carers and teachers!
The Rainbow Magic fairies are here to help your child enter the magical world of reading. Whatever reading stage they are at, there's a Rainbow Magic book for everyone! Here is Lydia the Reading Fairy's guide to supporting your child's journey at all levels.

1

Starting Out

Our Rainbow Magic Beginner Readers are perfect for first-time readers who are just beginning to develop reading skills and confidence. Approved by teachers, they contain a full range of educational levelling, as well as lively full-colour illustrations.

2

Developing Readers

Rainbow Magic Early Readers contain longer stories and wider vocabulary for building stamina and growing confidence. These are adaptations of our most popular Rainbow Magic stories, specially developed for younger readers in conjunction with an Early Years reading consultant, with full-colour illustrations.

3

Going Solo

The Rainbow Magic chapter books – a mixture of series and one-off specials – contain accessible writing to encourage your child to venture into reading independently. These highly collectible and much-loved magical stories inspire a love of reading to last a lifetime.

www.orchardseriesbooks.co.uk

"Rainbow Magic got my daughter reading chapter books. Great sparkly covers, cute fairies and traditional stories full of magic that she found impossible to put down" – Mother of Edie (6 years)

"Florence LOVES the Rainbow Magic books. She really enjoys reading now" – Mother of Florence (6 years)

Read along the Reading Rainbow!

Well done – you have completed the book!

This book was worth 1 star.

See how far you have climbed on the Reading Rainbow opposite.
The more books you read, the more stars you can colour in
and the closer you will be to becoming a Royal Fairy!

Do you want to print your own Reading Rainbow?

1) Go to the Rainbow Magic website

2) Download and print out the poster

3) Colour in a star for every book you finish
and climb the Reading Rainbow

4) For every step up the rainbow,
you can download your very own certificate

There's all this and lots more at

orchardseriesbooks.co.uk

You'll find activities, stories, a special newsletter
AND you can search for the fairy with your name!